# THE PIRATE GHOST

# Don't miss any of the cases in the Hardy Boys Clue Book series!

# HARDY BOYS

→ Clue Book ←

#7

## THE PIRATE GHOST

BY FRANKLIN W. DIXON ⟷ ILLUSTRATED BY SANTY GUTIÉRREZ

## ALADDIN

NEW YORK   LONDON   TORONTO   SYDNEY   NEW DELHI

# ALADDIN

An imprint of Simon & Schuster Children's Publishing Division
1230 Avenue of the Americas, New York, NY 10020
First Aladdin paperback edition April 2018
Text copyright © 2018 by Simon & Schuster, Inc.
Illustrations copyright © 2018 by Santy Gutiérrez
Also available in an Aladdin hardcover edition.

For information about special discounts for bulk purchases, please contact
Simon & Schuster Special Sales at 1-866-506-1949 or business@simonandschuster.com.
The Simon & Schuster Speakers Bureau can bring authors to your live event.
For more information or to book an event contact the Simon & Schuster Speakers Bureau
at 1-866-248-3049 or visit our website at www.simonspeakers.com.
Series designed by Karina Granda
Cover designed by Nina Simoneaux
The text of this book was set in Adobe Garamond Pro.
Manufactured in the United States of America 0318 OFF
2 4 6 8 10 9 7 5 3 1
Library of Congress Control Number 2017963812
ISBN 978-1-4814-8873-0 (hc)
ISBN 978-1-4814-8872-3 (pbk)
ISBN 978-1-4814-8874-7 (eBook)

# CONTENTS

# Chapter 1

# TALK AND SQUAWK

"Arrgh, you bilge-sucking scalawags!" Chet Morton growled. He lowered his pirate eye patch to give a wink. "All hands on doughnuts!"

Eight-year-old Joe was dressed like a pirate too in a puffy shirt. "How could pirates dig for buried treasure in itchy shirts like this?" he asked.

"It's Pirate Palooza Day in Bayport, Joe," Frank said as he straightened his pirate bandanna.

"Whoever comes to the festival after school dressed like a pirate—"

"Gets a free doughnut!" Chet said. "Bring it!"

It was Friday and the last day of school before spring break. Many kids dressed in pirate gear walked up and down Bay Street for the Pirate Palooza.

"I wonder what life was like in the days of pirates," Frank said. "Do you think there were detectives?"

Frank and Joe loved solving mysteries more than anything else. Their dad, Fenton Hardy, had his own detective agency in Bayport. The boys had something just as good: their own clue book, which Joe carried everywhere.

"If there were detectives back then," Joe said, scratching his itchy arm, "I hope they didn't dress like pirates!"

The boys checked out the cool festivities. Kids lined up to take pictures in the Pirate Photo Booth. A stand sold Swashbuckling Smoothies.

"I can't wait to see the Talk Like a Pirate Contest," Joe said. "I heard the prize is a map leading to a treasure chest buried right here in Bayport."

"A treas-arrrgh chest filled with doughnuts, I'll bet!" Chet growled in his best pirate voice. "Arrrgh!"

"Arrrk!" a nearby voice squawked.

"I said *arrrgh*, not *arrrk*," Chet pointed out.

Frank, Joe, and Chet turned to see Jason Wang from school. Jason was dressed like a pirate too, with something extra: his bright red-and-green parrot on his shoulder!

"Arrk!" the parrot squawked again. "Pirates ahoy, pirates ahoy—raaak!"

"Hey!" Frank said with a smile. "It's Crackers!"

Jason's pet parrot flapped his feathery wings. He not only talked—he could squawk a whole song after hearing it only once!

"Hi, guys," Jason greeted the others. "Crackers and I are here for the Talk Like a Pirate Contest."

"You mean 'squawk' like a pirate!" Joe laughed.

"Can we get our freebies already? Please?" Chet said impatiently.

"Onward, buccaneers," Joe declared, "to Double Doughnuts!"

But before the boys could head to the doughnut shop, four other kids walked over. Frank recognized Tobias Singh from another fourth-grade class.

"What's up, Tobias?" Frank said. He nodded at the red caps Tobias and his friends were wearing. "Those don't look like pirate hats."

"Yeah," Chet agreed. "Don't you guys want free doughnuts?"

Tobias pointed to the words on their matching red T-shirts: JUNIOR DIGGERS OF BAYPORT. "We're not here for the Pirate Palooza," he explained, his face serious. "We're here on business."

"'Junior Diggers,'" Chet read. "Isn't that the new snarky-ology club?"

"Archeology!" Tobias corrected.

Third grader Ava Carter explained, "We meet every week in Tobias's attic clubhouse. We then head out to dig up ancient relics in Bayport."

"Have you actually dug up old stuff in Bayport?" Joe asked. "Really, really old stuff?"

"Are you kidding me?" Tobias exclaimed. "We have a treasure chest in our clubhouse full of coins!"

"And an Egyptian mummy!" fourth grader Mikey Velasquez added.

"A mummy?" Chet repeated. "How do you find these things?"

"We know exactly where to dig," Tobias said. "Which is why we want to dig in Jason's backyard next."

"Wait a minute," Jason said, blinking with surprise. "Why my backyard?"

"Because centuries ago pirates sailed into Bayport," Tobias explained. "Once here, they would stay at the Peg-Leg Inn."

"Your house was built where the Peg-Leg Inn used to stand," third grader Lily Boyd said excitedly. "Think of all the pirate treasure we can dig up in your yard, Jason!"

Jason shook his head. "It's never going to happen."

"Why not?" Tobias asked.

"My parents are neat freaks when it comes to our lawns," Jason explained. "My mom won't even let me dig for worms for Crackers."

"Bummer, bummer," Crackers screeched. "Raaak!"

"Besides," Jason said, "I never found any pirate stuff around my house anyway."

"How do we know for sure there even was a Peg-Leg Inn?" Joe asked.

"Well, no one knows for sure, but that rumor has been around for a long time. Maybe the pirates stayed at the Bayport Motel instead," Chet said. "At least the motel has a pool and Wi-Fi!"

"So the answer is no?" Tobias asked Jason.

"Sorry," Jason said.

"Yeah, sure, you are," Tobias muttered before leading the other club members away. A few glanced over their shoulders to frown at Jason.

"Definitely not happy campers," Jason sighed.

"You mean diggers," Joe said.

Suddenly—

"Raaaak!" Crackers screeched. He spread his feathery wings and took off!

"Crackers!" Jason cried as his parrot flapped away. "Get back here—now!"

The boys ran in Crackers's direction, but the parrot disappeared into the crowd.

"Where'd he go?" Frank asked.

"Back off, birdie!!" a girl's angry voice shouted from the crowd. "I said vamoose, pellet breath!"

Frank, Joe, Chet, and Jason followed the voice through the crowd until they saw Crackers. The parrot hovered in midair above a frantic girl.

"That's Reilly Voorhees from school!" Joe said.

"She's the star of all the class plays," Frank added.

Reilly dressed like a star too. Today she wore a sparkly silver-and-red pirate costume with glittery silver tap shoes.

"Crackers!" Jason yelled. He held out his arm.

"It's okay, Reilly," Joe said as Crackers landed on Jason's arm. "Jason told us that parrots like shiny things."

"Crackers and I are in the Talk Like a Pirate Contest," Jason added as Crackers preened on his arm. "Pretty cool, huh?"

"Not cool!" Reilly snapped. "I'll bet pets aren't allowed in the contest because they would steal the show!"

"I guess that's up to the judge to decide," Frank said with a shrug.

"And that, laddie," a deep, gravelly voice piped up, "would be your-rrrrghs truly!"

Who'd said that? The kids turned and gasped. Standing behind them was a stubbly-bearded pirate. On his head was a pirate hat. Over one eye was a black patch.

"Pirates ahoy, pirates ahoy!" Crackers screeched. "Arrrk!"

"The feathery flapper is correct, mateys," the pirate said. "I've sailed around the coast of Florida-arrrrgh, the shores of Canada-arrrrrgh—even the seas of Africa-arrrgh for treasure-arrrgh!"

The boys and Reilly stared at the pirate.

"Um," Frank said, "do we know you?"

The pirate took a sweeping bow. "The name is Plunderin' Pete," he growled. "Teller of tall tales and judge of the Talk Like a Pirate Contest."

"A pirate is judging a pirate contest?" Joe asked. "Awesome."

"You're going to love my song-and-dance number,

Pirate Pete," Reilly said as she began tapping her feet. "It's not just good—it's spectacul-arrrrgh!"

Chet ignored Reilly as he asked, "Were there really pirates in Bayport, Pete?"

"There were and still are-rrgh!" Plunderin' Pete replied. "Haven't you heard about the notorious Captain Scurvydog?"

"Captain Scurvydog?" Jason asked.

Reilly stopping tapping to ask, "Who's he?"

"About three hundred years ago Captain Scurvydog made Bayport his port of call," Plunderin' Pete explained. "He fancied the town and decided to come back . . . and back . . . and back . . . to this very day."

"To this very day?" Frank repeated.

"You mean," Joe asked slowly, "Captain Scurvydog is a ghost?"

# GHOST TOWN

At the word "ghost," Plunderin' Pete's one uncovered eye lit up. "Aye!" he said. "The ghost of Captain Scurvydog comes back to make sure buried treasure isn't dug up by landlubbing scoundrels."

"Buried treasure?" asked Reilly. "You mean like the prize for the Talk Like a Pirate Contest?"

"Buried treasure is buried treas-arrrrgh, lass," Pete replied.

"Polish yer doubloons, matey!" Crackers screeched. "Arrrk!"

"Doubloons?" Reilly asked. "What's he squawking about?"

"Doubloons were ancient Spanish gold coins," Jason explained.

"Gold coins to them," Plunderin' Pete cackled. "Pirate booty to me!"

But Chet was interested in something else. He tilted his head as he studied Plunderin' Pete. "This Captain Scurvydog," he said. "Is he a good ghost or a bad ghost?"

"Scurvydog is a good ghost," Pete answered.

"That's a relief," said Chet. "I was afraid he—"

"Until someone digs up a pirate's treasure," Pete cut in. "Then pity the poor soul who faces Scurvydog's wrath!"

All the kids stared at Plunderin' Pete.

"And now, me hearties," Pete growled with a smile, "it's time for this pirate to claim his free doughnut."

Plunderin' Pete adjusted his eye patch, then headed toward the doughnut shop.

"Just great," Chet complained. "I'll bet he'll get the last Bavarian cream."

"Who cares about doughnuts?" Jason exclaimed. "There's a ghost named Captain Scurvydog around, and he's a mean dude!"

"Don't worry, Jason," Frank said. "The buried treasure in the contest can't be cursed."

"Yeah, it's not like the treasure chest will have pirate booty inside," Joe told Jason. "Probably stretchy frogs and tubs of slime."

"You guys!" Reilly piped up. "Jason does not have to worry about the buried treasure."

"Why not?" Jason asked.

"Because," Reilly said, jutting her chin out, "I'm going to win the Talk Like a Pirate Contest—not you!"

Reilly turned and walked away, her sparkly shoes tapping on the sidewalk as she went.

"How do you say 'diva' in pirate talk?" Chet complained.

"It's okay," Jason said with a small smile. "I don't believe in ghosts. Not really."

The boys went to get their doughnuts. They also got to check out more Pirate Palooza activities, like a pirate stick-on tattoo booth, a sponge sword fight, pirate jewelry crafts, and more tall tales by Plunderin' Pete.

But soon came the event everyone was waiting for—the Talk Like a Pirate Contest!

"Break a peg leg!" Joe called to Jason as he and Crackers hurried to join the other contestants.

Frank, Joe, and Chet squeezed through the crowd near the stage that had been set up for the contest. Hector Alvarez, the owner of Double Doughnuts, was stepping up to the microphone.

"Ahoy, Bayport Buccaneers!" Hector boomed. "Let's raise the roof and a Jolly Roger flag for our first pirate-talking contestant—Phil Cohen!"

The Hardys' friend Phil ran onto the stage. Talking like a pirate, he described his latest pirate invention: a gadget for detecting metals and buried treasure.

"Arrgh," Phil growled as the gadget beeped over a coin dropped onto the stage floor. "Be the first on your galleon to own this dead-reckoning thingamajig!"

"Woo-hoo!" Joe cheered for their friend.

Next up was Chet's sister, Iola Morton. Her imitation of a pirate principal got big laughs and applause.

"There will be no substitute teachers walking the plank," Iola declared. "And no stashing doubloons in your gym lock-arrrrghs!"

"I kind of hope she wins," Chet admitted to

Frank and Joe as his sister left the stage. "I heard there's candy in that treasure chest."

More pirate talkers took the stage. Finally it was Jason's turn with his collection of pirate jokes. . . .

"Hey, Crack-arrrghs. What did Captain Hook get on his report carrrrd?" asked Jason.

"Raaak!" Crackers answered, rolling his feathery neck. "High *C*s, high *C*s!"

"Crack-arrrghs?" Jason asked next. "Why can't pirates play carrrrds?"

"Arrk!" Crackers squawked. "Because they're always standing on decks."

Joe could see Plunderin' Pete laughing at Jason's jokes. It was no surprise that Jason and Crackers got the biggest cheers as they left the stage.

"Who can top that?" Joe asked.

"Maybe her?" Frank said.

Music blared as Reilly tap-tapped onstage. She was followed by more dancing kids dressed in sparkly pirate costumes too.

"Cheese and crackers!" Chet exclaimed. "It's like she brought her whole dance class!"

Reilly's feet were a blur as she tapped across the linoleum dance floor laid out just for her. Spreading her arms, she began to sing, "Why walk the plank? Kick up your heels and dance instead!"

The chorus of dancing pirates tapped behind Reilly as she belted out her song. After the big finish, Reilly took a bow. She then pretended to be surprised when her little brother Sam walked onstage with a bouquet of roses.

"Thank you, Reilly Voorhees," Hector said as the dancers tapped offstage. "It won't be easy, but it's time for Plunderin' Pete to pick the winner."

Plunderin' Pete grabbed the mike. Gazing at the audience with one eye, he growled, "And the win-arrrgh is . . . Jason and his first mate, Crackers!"

Frank, Joe, and Chet let out a cheer as Jason ran to Pete with Crackers on his shoulder.

"Congratulations, me hearties," Pete said. "For talking like a pirate, here's the map to buried treas-arrrgh in Bayport!"

Gratefully Jason took the scroll. Crackers

stretched his neck to peck the shiny gold ribbon wrapped around it.

"And here's something from me," Plunderin' Pete told Jason. "A treas-arrrgh bag filled with more pirate booty!"

Pete handed Jason a red bag, a skull-and-crossbones design splashed on the front. "And rememb-arrrgh. Watch out for the notorious Captain Scurvydog!"

Jason shot Frank and Joe a grin. He then looked at Plunderin' Pete and said, "Thanks, but I don't believe in ghosts."

"Don't believe in ghosts?" Plunderin' Pete declared, his smile turning into a frown. "Well . . . shiver me timbers!"

"Uh-oh," Crackers squawked. "Arrrk!"

Holding his prizes, Jason ran off the stage. "I won, I won!" he shouted happily as he raced toward Frank and Joe. Chet had already left to say hi to his sister.

"Congrats, dude!" Frank said.

"You and Crackers rocked the contest!" Joe exclaimed.

"You mean stole the show!" Reilly snapped as she stormed over. "Pets should not have been in the contest!"

"Jason and Crackers won fair and square, Reilly," Frank said.

Reilly narrowed her eyes directly at Jason. "Who wants a haunted treasure map anyway?" she demanded. "Say hello to the ghost of Captain Scurvydog, Jason!"

Jason's eyes popped wide open as Reilly huffed off.

"Don't listen to what Reilly said, Jason," Frank said.

"Yeah," Joe said, "You don't believe in ghosts anyway, right?"

"Right," Jason said slowly. He then turned to the brothers and said, "Tomorrow's Saturday. Why don't you come to my house then and help me dig up the treasure chest?"

"We're there!" Joe exclaimed.

"Thanks, Jason," Frank said.

Joe wanted to peek inside the pirate treasure bag, but Jason spotted his parents and ran off.

"Dude, we're digging for buried treasure tomorrow," Frank told Joe excitedly. "What do you say about that?"

"Two words," Joe declared. "Pirates ahoy!"

"Sounds like the Pirate Palooza was a real lollapalooza," Fenton Hardy said, placing a pile of dirty dinner dishes on the kitchen counter.

Frank rinsed the dishes while Joe loaded the dishwasher. They'd spent most of dinner talking about the Pirate Palooza and the Talk Like a Pirate Contest.

"It was awesome, Dad," Frank said, scraping pasta sauce off a dish. "You should have seen Jason and Crackers's comedy act. It brought down the house!"

"Speaking of house," Joe said, looking up from the dish he was about to load. "Mom, do you know anything about the house you sold to Jason's family?"

Laura Hardy was a real estate agent. She knew about most of the houses in Bayport. "Only that it has three bedrooms, an eat-in kitchen," she said, "plus a huge backyard perfect for gardening."

"Was it also built where an old pirate inn stood hundreds of years ago?" Frank asked. "That's what the Junior Diggers told Jason."

"Why don't I research the house when I'm back at work?" Mrs. Hardy said. "I'll let you guys know."

"Thanks, Mom," Joe said.

"So what time is your big buried-treasure dig tomorrow?" Mr. Hardy asked.

"Good question, Dad," Frank said after trading shrugs with Joe. "We forgot to ask Jason."

Mrs. Hardy held out a small red book she used for work. "The Wangs' number should be in here," she said. "Why don't you give Jason a call?"

Joe took the book, found the Wangs' phone number, and dialed it on the kitchen phone. After three rings Jason picked up and said hello.

"Hey, Jason," Joe said cheerily. "So what time should Frank and I drop by tomorrow—"

"Don't!" Jason's voice snapped.

"Huh?" Joe shot Frank a puzzled look. Quickly

he put the phone on speaker and asked, "Don't what, Jason?"

"Don't come tomorrow," Jason blurted frantically. "I'm not digging for treasure—any treasure!"

Frank leaned toward the phone and asked, "What do you mean you're not digging for treasure?"

The brothers waited for Jason's answer. Instead they heard a click. Jason had hung up!

# Chapter 3

## SHIVERY DELIVERY

The next morning Frank and Joe headed to the Wangs' house. They still had no clue why Jason had canceled the dig. When they reached Jason's house, they found him standing on the porch next to Crackers's cage.

"Eat 'em up, eat 'em up!" Crackers squawked as Jason squeezed cut-up celery sticks through the cage bars.

"I had a feeling you'd come over today," Jason said to the Hardys. "I told you guys, the dig is off."

"Yeah, but you didn't tell us why," Joe said.

"What's up?" Frank asked. "Don't you want to dig up your prize?"

"I want to dig," Jason insisted. "But someone else doesn't want me to."

"Who?" Joe asked. "Your mom? Your dad?"

Jason turned away from the cage, looking nervous. "It was the ghost," he said in almost a whisper. "The ghost of Captain Scurvydog!"

Frank and Joe stared wide-eyed at Jason. Had they just heard what they thought they'd heard?

"What makes you think it's a ghost, Jason?" Frank asked slowly.

"And don't leave out a thing," Joe added.

Jason stepped away from Crackers's cage toward Frank and Joe. "Last night my parents took me out for pizza to celebrate my win," he explained.

"Pepperoni?" Joe asked.

"Mushroom and cheese," Jason replied. "When we got back home, my parents went inside, but I stayed out here to say hi to Crackers."

Jason shook his head as he added, "The moment

I got near the cage, I could tell that Crackers . . . had gone crackers."

"What do you mean?" Frank asked.

"He started singing a song I never taught him," Jason said. "It sounded like—"

Before Jason could explain, Crackers began to sing, "Windy weather, boys, stormy weather, boys. When the wind blows, we're all together, boys. Raak!"

"That's it!" Jason said. "That's the song!"

"Sounds like an old pirate song to me," Frank said. "Are you sure you never taught Crackers the song, Jason?"

"Sure I'm sure," Jason insisted. "Who else could teach an old pirate song to Crackers but the ghost of an old pirate?"

"Anybody could have taught him that song, though," Frank answered.

"Sure," Joe agreed. "Someone could have walked up to his cage on the porch while you and your parents were at the pizza place."

Jason shook his head and said, "There's more."

"More?" Joe and Frank asked at the same time.

"I found that on our doorstep last night," Jason said, pointing to a blue bottle standing near the door, "with a message inside!"

"Wow!" Joe exclaimed. He had heard about messages in bottles floating in the sea—but what was one doing on Jason's front porch?

"What did the message say?" Frank asked.

Jason flipped the bottle upside down. A tightly rolled-up sheet of paper dropped out. Jason unrolled it and handed it to Frank. "Read it yourself," he said.

Joe looked over Frank's shoulder as he read the message out loud: "'Hands off the buried treasure. Signed, CS.'"

The brothers studied the note. The message was written very plainly in block letters with black ink.

"You think *CS* stands for 'Captain Scurvydog'?" Joe asked.

"Well, it doesn't stand for 'chocolate sprinkles,'" Jason said sarcastically as he grabbed the message back. "But there's more."

Frank and Joe traded surprised looks. With so many mysterious clues, no wonder Jason needed their help!

"I found these on my windowsill last night," Jason said as he pulled a handful of coins from his pocket.

The brothers studied the golden-colored coins in Jason's palm. Each small, flat coin had uneven edges and was stamped with an old-timey sailing ship on one side and a Jolly Roger flag on the other. The black flag with a skull-and-crossbones design had been flown by pirates hundreds of years ago.

Frank took one coin from Jason. "Looks like pirate booty to me," he decided, turning it over in his own hand.

"The coins were another sign from Captain Scurvydog's ghost," Jason said, stuffing the coins back into his pocket. "He's warning me not to dig up buried treasure!"

"So you're not going to use the treasure map you won in the contest?" Joe asked. "You said you didn't believe in ghosts, Jason!"

"I didn't," Jason said, "until now."

Jason turned to swat a bee away from Crackers's cage. Frank and Joe stepped away to discuss what they'd just heard.

"Jason totally believes in that pirate ghost," Frank whispered. "How are we ever going to change his mind?"

"There's only one way," Joe said with a smile. He pulled their clue book from his pocket and sang, "Ta-da!"

"What are you guys doing?" Jason asked.

"We want to figure out who left that weird pirate stuff around your house, Jason," Frank said, "and taught Crackers that song."

"And we don't think it's Captain Scurvydog!" Joe declared.

"Who else could it be?" Jason asked.

"We think someone is trying to scare you," Frank explained. "Maybe someone who wanted to win the Talk Like a Pirate Contest."

"Can Frank and I take some pirate coins with us as clues, Jason?" Joe asked. "Or the message in a bottle?"

"Maybe we can study the handwriting in the message—" Frank started to say, before Jason firmly shook his head.

"No way," Jason said. "I know you guys are detectives, but don't make this one of your cases."

"Why not?" Frank asked.

"Because," Jason replied, turning toward the door. "You might upset the ghost of Captain Scurvydog!"

Without a good-bye, he entered the house and shut the door.

Joe heaved a big sigh and said, "Our bud Jason is going to be a tough nut to crack."

"Which is why we have to crack this case anyway," Frank stated. "Let's get to work!"

Joe opened the clue book. Tucked inside was his favorite pen, which was also a mini flashlight. After turning to a clean page, he wrote: *Pirate Ghost—or Pirate Hoax?*

"Let's look for more clues while we're still here," Frank suggested. "Then we'll figure out who could be scaring Jason."

Crackers suddenly squawked and began to sing, "Congratulations, Jason! You're pirate number one! And with that awesome treasure map . . . treasure map . . . treasure map . . ."

Crackers's singing voice trailed off as the brothers stared into his cage.

"That doesn't sound like an old pirate song to me," Frank said.

"I guess Crackers has a long playlist!" said Joe.

The brothers walked to the doorstep, where Jason had found the message in the bottle. Looking down, they noticed gold-colored specks shimmering from the floorboards.

"Since when do ghosts leave pixie dust?" Joe asked.

"It's glitter, Joe," Frank said, "and a great clue."

Joe wrote the clue in his book. "Let's check out Jason's window where he found those gold coins."

The brothers headed around the house to Jason's bedroom window.

"Jason's window isn't very high," Joe pointed out. "Any kid could have put the pirate coins on his windowsill."

Frank had pocketed the one coin that Jason had let him see. He held it up and said, "But who has old-looking coins like this?"

"Yeah," Joe said, studying the coin. "It looks like they were dug up somewhere."

Dug up? Frank's eyes lit up.

"Joe," he said excitedly. "The Junior Diggers of Bayport bragged about some treasure chest full of coins they had, remember?"

"How could I forget?" Joe asked. "They wanted to dig for ancient pirate stuff in Jason's backyard!" He smiled as he wrote the club's name in the clue book. "I think we have our first suspects. The Junior Diggers of Bayport!"

"Good work so far," Frank declared. "What should we look for next?"

"A place to have lunch," Joe said, shutting the clue book, "before my stomach growls more than Plunderin' Pete!"

When the boys went home to ask their mom about lunch, Mrs. Hardy offered to drop Frank and Joe off at one of their favorite places: Beefy Burger. The burger place was packed with kids celebrating the first day of spring break.

"I'll pick you boys up in a bit," Mrs. Hardy said

as she parked outside the restaurant. "Have fun!"

Walking toward the food counter, the brothers saw something popping up from the crowd of diners. Something yellow with floppy green leaves.

"It's a pineapple!" Frank said.

"Pineapple burger?" asked Joe.

"No," Frank said. "A pineapple hat!"

The boys noticed something else. Wearing the pineapple hat was Reilly Voorhees!

Reilly sat at a small table with her friend Paisley Horner. Reilly wore another dance costume and a supersize pineapple on her head. But what really caught the brothers' eyes was what she had on her feet!

"Reilly is wearing gold shoes," Frank whispered. "And they look glittery to me."

"Like the glitter we found by Jason's doorstep!" Joe whispered back.

The brothers walked slowly past the girls' table. Reilly Voorhees was the star of the class plays. Was she also Jason's pirate ghost?

# Chapter 4

# THAR SHE GLOWS!

The brothers slipped into the food line. With their backs turned to Reilly, they strained their ears to listen.

"I can't believe I had to go to Jason Wang's house yesterday after the contest," Reilly was saying.

"Why did you have to go there?" Paisley asked. "Especially after he won the contest and you didn't."

"Paisley, do you have to remind me?" Reilly complained. "I went to Jason's house to give him a message, okay?"

Message?

"Frank!" Joe whispered. "Maybe Reilly's talking about that message in the bottle Jason found!"

"Reilly was mad at Jason for winning," Frank whispered, "and for Crackers stealing the show."

"So she had a reason to leave that pirate stuff to scare Jason," Joe whispered. "Dad would call that a motive."

Frank and Joe looked back over their shoulders. Reilly and Paisley were standing up.

"Should we go to Mandy's Candy next?" Paisley asked. "They're giving out free glow-in-the-dark bubble gum today."

"Can't," Reilly said, her pineapple wobbling as she shook her head. "I have another message to deliver."

The friends returned their trays and left Beefy Burger. Joe turned to Frank and said, "Did you hear that? Reilly said she's delivering another message!"

"It could be another message to Jason," Frank said.

"I've got a message for you guys!" a boy standing

behind them in line said. "Keep the line moving before the burgers get cold and crusty!"

Instead of inching toward the burgers, Frank stepped out of the line.

"What about our burgers, Frank?" Joe asked.

"Forget about the burgers," Frank said. "And follow that pineapple!"

Frank and Joe returned their empty trays and left Beefy Burger. They looked around for Reilly and didn't see her. They did see something else, though.

"Look!" Frank said, pointing down. "There's gold glitter on the sidewalk."

Joe noticed more glittery speckles up the block. "There's a trail of it," he said. "Let's follow it and see where it leads."

They followed the trail around the corner. Looking up the block, they saw the giant pineapple and Reilly!

"Reilly's on Jason's block," Frank whispered.

Joe stopped to write Reilly's name on his suspect list. "If Reilly is leaving Jason secret messages," he asked, "why would she wear a pineapple hat? It draws a lot of attention."

The brothers saw Reilly stop halfway up the block. She turned toward a blue house with white shutters and walked up the path to the door.

"That's not Jason's house," Frank said. "Where's she going?"

Joe and Frank inched toward the house. Reilly stood on the doorstep, ringing the bell. After a few seconds the door was opened by a woman who smiled at Reilly.

"Well, what a surprise!" the woman said loudly. She then glanced over her shoulder and shouted into the house, "Honey—someone sent us a Pineapple Gram!"

"Pineapple Gram?" Joe whispered.

"What's a Pineapple Gram?" Frank whispered too.

A man appeared at the door. Reilly began tap-dancing on the doorstep as she sang, "Happy fifth anniversary, from Grandpa Lee. Please save some cake for your little ol' pineapple—me!"

Frank and Joe exchanged stunned looks. Was this the kind of message Reilly had spoken about?

"Wait right here!" the man said cheerily before

ducking into the house. He came back with a cake slice and a fork on a paper plate.

After the door closed, the boys hurried up to Reilly. Not looking up from her plate, she said, "Sorry, but you can't have a piece of cake. I worked hard for this slice."

"We don't want cake," Joe said. "We want to ask you a few things."

"You mean about the pineapple on my head?" Reilly asked with a smile. "It's the costume I wear when I deliver singing telegrams after school and on weekends."

"Telegrams?" asked Joe.

"I call them Pineapple Grams," Reilly said. "They're awesome practice for my big stage career. And as you can see, the pay is yummy!"

Frank and Joe followed Reilly away from the house.

"Weird things happened at Jason Wang's house last night," Joe said.

"We found gold glitter on his doorstep," Frank added, "and a message in a bottle."

"So?" Reilly asked.

"So we heard you say you delivered a message to Jason last night," Frank replied.

Reilly rolled her eyes. "I did deliver a message," she said. "A Pineapple Gram message!"

Frank and Joe stared at Reilly.

"You mean one of those singing things?" Joe asked.

"Yes," Reilly said. "Jason's parents ordered one to congratulate him for winning the contest."

"So you didn't leave a message in a bottle?" Joe asked slowly. "Or a bunch of old pirate coins?"

"And you didn't teach Crackers a pirate song either?" Frank added.

"I wouldn't go near that nutty bird," Reilly huffed. "Especially with shiny shoes like these!"

As Reilly walked away, Frank whispered to Joe, "How do we know Reilly is telling the truth about that Pineapple Gram?"

Joe wasn't sure until an idea popped into his head. "Hey, Reilly!" he shouted. "How about another song?"

# Chapter 5

# HOLE LOT OF CLUE!

"Joe, what are you doing?" Frank hissed as they hurried over to Reilly. "I don't want to hear another one of her songs."

"You might want to hear this one," Joe whispered.

Reilly looked up from her cake as the boys approached. "If it's a Pineapple Gram you want," she told them, "it'll cost you a piece of cake."

"We don't want a Pineapple Gram," Joe explained.

"We just want to hear the song you sang for Jason last night."

Reilly wrinkled her nose and said, "Why?"

Joe didn't want to tell Reilly the real reason. So he forced himself to say, "Um . . . because your songs are . . . awesome?"

"Well, if you put it that way," Reilly said with a smile. She threw back her shoulders and began to sing, "Congratulations, Jason! You're pirate number one! And with that awesome treasure map, the fun has just begun!"

Joe shot Frank a sideways glance. That was the same song Crackers had sung for them that morning!

"I follow every song with a dance," Reilly said. But before she could start tapping—

"It's okay, Reilly!" Joe cut in. "The song was . . . awesome enough."

"Thanks," said Reilly. Her pineapple hat wobbled as she walked away.

The brothers waited until Reilly was out of ear-shot. Frank then turned to Joe and said, "Crackers sang Reilly's song! He must have heard her sing it to Jason last night!"

"So Reilly's message wasn't the message in the bottle," Joe weighed in. "It was her Pineapple Gram."

"Could Reilly have stuck around after her Pineapple Gram?" Frank wondered. "To leave the bottle and coins and teach Crackers that song?"

"No way," Joe said, shaking his head. "You heard what Reilly said about Crackers."

"Yeah," Frank chuckled. "She probably couldn't leave the Wang house fast enough!"

Joe crossed Reilly's name off the suspect list. "Reilly Voorhees is no longer a singing suspect," he said.

Frank looked up the block. "Jason lives a few houses down," he said. "Let's tell him what we know so far."

The brothers made their way to Jason's house. Crackers squawked from his cage on the porch while Frank rang the doorbell. By the third ring, the brothers decided the Wangs were not home.

"It's Saturday," Joe said as they turned away from the door. "Maybe they went to the movies or—"

"Dig 'em up! Dig 'em up!" Crackers screeched.

Frank and Joe turned toward the parrot's cage. Crackers bobbed his head up and down as he squawked, "Dig 'em up, dig 'em up. Ooh boy!"

"Dig 'em up?" Frank said as he and Joe approached the parrot's cage. "What's that mean?"

Joe peered into Crackers's cage and smiled. "I want to know if that bell made out of birdseeds really rings!" he said.

"Joe, don't open the cage door!" Frank warned.

Too late. The second Joe opened the door, Crackers squeezed through. He hopped onto Joe's arm, spread his colorful wings, and took off!

"No, Crackers, no!" Joe shouted after the fly-away parrot. "Come back!"

"I told you not to open the cage!" Frank said as they chased Crackers around the house.

"Where'd he go?" Joe cried as he and Frank raced into the Wangs' yard.

"There!" said Frank, pointing toward the back of the yard. Sitting atop a tree branch was Crackers!

The brothers ran to the tree and the parrot.

"Great," Frank groaned. "How are we going to get him back into his cage?"

"Wait, look over here!" said Joe excitedly.

Frank looked to see where his brother was pointing. On the ground below the branch was a freshly dug hole.

"An animal could have made that," Frank said.

"Would an animal wear a hat?" Joe asked.

"Huh?" said Frank.

Joe walked toward a red cap stuck on the twig of a nearby hedge. "This cap looks familiar," he said. "Where did we see it before?"

"Dig 'em up! Dig 'em up!" Crackers squawked.

Dig 'em up?

The brothers looked at the red cap, then at the hole in the ground. That was when it suddenly clicked!

"Hey, Frank," Joe said. "I think our feathered friend is trying to tell us something."

Crackers looked satisfied as he hopped back into his cage.

# Chapter 6

# FOLLOW THAT BEEP!

"The Junior Diggers of Bayport wore red caps like this," Frank said. "They could have left the pirate clues around the place to scare Jason."

"And after they left the clues," Joe said, pointing at the hole in the ground, "they could have stuck around for a quick dig as the last straw!"

"Tobias and his club are already suspects," Frank said. "But Dad always says we should get as much evidence as possible before accusing anyone."

"In that case," Joe said as he grabbed the cap and put it on, "let's go to their clubhouse to dig around for clues."

Tobias lived only three blocks away from Jason's house. When Frank and Joe rang the bell, the door was opened by Mrs. Singh.

"Hi, boys," Mrs. Singh said with a smile. "If you're here to visit Tobias, he and his club went out on a dig."

"Can we wait for them, please?" Frank asked.

"In the clubhouse?" Joe blurted quickly.

"I'm pretty sure Tobias's clubhouse is for members only," Mrs. Singh said, but she smiled when she noticed Joe's cap. "I can see that you're a member too, so go on up."

"Thanks, Mrs. Singh!" Joe exclaimed.

Mrs. Singh led the boys into the house. "You know where the stairs are," she said, pointing to a staircase at the end of a hallway. "Tobias and the others should be home pretty soon."

"Not too soon, I hope," Joe told Frank softly as they climbed the stairs. "We need to check out the clubhouse for clues!"

Frank and Joe reached the top of the stairs and stepped into the attic. What they saw made their jaws drop.

"Holy cannoli!" Joe gasped.

"Look at all this neat stuff!" Frank exclaimed.

All around were old-timey relics from Bayport: a ship's steering wheel, a yellowing map of Bayport, plus shelves full of dusty old bottles of colored glass.

"That's where they could have gotten the blue bottle!" Joe pointed out excitedly.

Frank turned toward a tall, oblong case leaning against the wall. "There's the mummy Tobias told us about," he said. "It must be inside that sarcophagus."

"Sar-koff-a-gus," Joe pronounced carefully. "How do you know so much about mummies, Frank?"

"We learned about ancient Egypt in history," Frank answered. "But what's an ancient Egyptian mummy doing in Bayport?"

As he headed toward the sarcophagus, Joe called out, "Hey, Frank, look at this!" Frank turned to see Joe holding a long sticklike device. It had a handle on one end and a wheel on the other.

"Isn't that the metal detector Phil invented?" Frank asked.

Joe nodded. "The Junior Diggers must have talked Phil into giving it to them," he said, "so they could use it to find more ancient stuff."

After pulling a penny from his pocket, Joe dropped it onto the floor. "Let's see if it still works," he said.

Frank watched as his brother waved the device over the penny. As it began to beep, he said, "It works, all right."

"It's fun, too!" Joe said. He waved the rod back and forth as he walked around the attic.

"Joe, put that away," Frank said. "We have to look for—"

*BEEEEEP! BEEP! BEEP!*

"The metal detector found something else, Frank," Joe said. "I wonder what."

He continued walking around the attic with the device, moving it back and forth. It beeped wildly as he approached something big and bulky. It looked like a box underneath a Jolly Roger flag.

"What's in there?" Frank wondered.

"Good question," Joe said. He put aside the metal detector and pulled off the flag. The box underneath looked exactly like—

"A treasure chest!" Joe exclaimed.

"What are we waiting for?" Frank said. "Let's open it!"

The brothers knelt next to the treasure chest. Together they took hold of the heavy lid and lifted it.

"Whoa!" Joe exclaimed as they peered inside.

"Check it out!" Frank said under his breath.

The chest was filled practically to the brim with coins. Golden, ancient-looking coins!

## YO HO—OH NO!

"Take out the coin Jason found on his windowsill, Frank," Joe said, "so we can compare it to these."

"Check," Frank said. He was about to reach for the coin when voices rose from the bottom of the staircase.

"It sounds like Tobias and his club are back!" Joe hissed. "We've got to hide!"

"Why?" Frank asked. "Mrs. Singh knows we're up here."

"She knows we're here to wait for the club," Joe whispered. "She doesn't know we're here to snoop!"

Joe rushed over to the mummy sarcophagus. "There's probably room in there for both of us," he said. "And the mummy, of course."

"Are you nutso?" Frank said, running after him. "It's dangerous to hide in there!"

"Maybe it's not a sarcophagus," Joe said.

"Huh?" Frank cried.

"Maybe it's a secret door leading somewhere else!" Joe said. He grabbed the edge of the sarcophagus lid and began to pull. The lid popped open and—

"Ahhhhh!" they both yelled as a tall, bandaged mummy tumbled out and pinned them both to the ground.

Through the chaos, Joe's cap flew off his head. As the brothers tried to roll the mummy off, the Junior Diggers of Bayport rushed over.

"My mom said you guys were up here, but what are you doing with our mummy?" Tobias demanded.

Frank and Joe dragged themselves out from underneath the mummy.

"What are you doing with an Egyptian mummy in your clubhouse?" Joe asked as he and Frank stood up. "Don't tell me you found it in Bayport."

"We totally found it here," Tobias insisted. "It was at the Bayport Fun Fair before they tore it down."

"A fun fair?" Joe asked. "So the mummy is really a dummy?"

"It's not ancient?" Frank asked.

"Nope," Lily said, waving the musty smell from her nose, "it just smells that way."

Lily and Mikey lifted the mummy, leaning it back inside the sarcophagus. Tobias patted the side of the sarcophagus proudly and said, "You guys would be surprised how many treasures can be found in Bayport."

"Speaking of treasures," Frank said, nodding toward the treasure chest. "Jason Wang found coins on his windowsill last night. Coins like the ones in there."

"And we found a hole in the Wangs' backyard,"

Joe added. He pointed to the red cap on the floor. "Plus that!"

Mikey smiled as he picked up the cap. "So that's where I lost my club cap."

"Aha!" Joe exclaimed. "So you guys were digging at Jason's house."

"After he said you couldn't," Frank added. "What's with you guys?"

The club members traded guilty glances.

"We were going to ask Jason's parents," Tobias admitted. "But nobody was home."

"Except that crazy bird," Lily said with a frown.

"We figured it would be okay to look for old pirate stuff above the ground," Tobias said. "But we're diggers, so we couldn't help ourselves!"

"Did you also leave pirate stuff around the house?" Frank asked.

"You told Jason his house was built over the old Peg-Leg Inn," Joe added. "Maybe you tried to scare him into believing there were pirate ghosts still hanging around!"

The club members shook their heads no.

"We were the ones who were scared," Mikey admitted. "That parrot started singing some creepy old pirate song."

"So we left," Tobias put in.

"Then what about that treasure chest of coins?" Joe asked. "Where did you get that?"

"Take a closer look at the coins and see for yourself," Tobias said.

Frank and Joe scooped up handfuls of coins, checking several at random. Each one was stamped with Tobias's face on one side, a saying on the other. . . .

"'Tobias Singh—Good as Gold'?" Frank read.

"That doesn't sound very ancient," Joe said.

"It's not," Tobias confessed. "The coins were from my birthday party last month. The theme was archeology."

"Cool," Frank admitted.

"Most of it was," Tobias said. "Except, where do you put candles on a pyramid-shaped cake?"

The Hardys tossed Tobias's birthday coins back into the treasure chest. They did not match the coins Jason had found on his windowsill.

"Does this mean we're clean?" Tobias asked.

"Yeah," Joe joked. "But your hands are covered with dirt!"

Frank smiled as the Junior Diggers frowned at their muddy hands. "Thanks for your help," he said. "Did you find something cool on your dig today?"

"Just some kid's retainer," Lily said.

"We're hoping it belonged to King Tut!" Tobias added with a grin.

Frank and Joe said good-bye to the diggers and Mrs. Singh. As they walked away from the house, Joe crossed the Junior Diggers off the suspect list.

"I'm glad Tobias and his club are innocent," he admitted. "But they were our last suspects, and we're back to square one."

"Yeah," Frank sighed. "Who could have put all that pirate stuff around Jason's house? And taught Crackers that song?"

Joe stared at his brother. "Maybe Jason's house really was built over an old pirate inn," he said. "Maybe it really is haunted like Jason thinks."

"If that's true," Frank said with a smirk, "then Captain Scurvydog wouldn't be the only ghost dropping by to say 'Boo!'"

"Mom, Dad," Joe said later that day as he carried a platter of corn into the Hardys' backyard. "This corn on the cob reminds me of a joke Jason and Crackers told at the Pirate Palooza."

Frank looked up from placing plates on the picnic table. It was a warm spring evening, and the Hardys were having their first barbecue of the year. "Which joke?" he asked.

"Okay," Joe said, cracking a smile. "What do pirates pay for corn on the cob?"

"You got me," Mr. Hardy said as he fired up the grill. "What do pirates pay for corn on the cob?"

"Yes, what?" Mrs. Hardy asked, walking by with a platter of hamburger patties and veggie kebobs.

"A buck an ear!" Joe laughed. "Buccaneer . . . get it?"

"Corny!" Frank teased. "But that joke did help Jason win the Talk Like a Pirate Contest."

"And speaking of Jason, boys," their mom said with a smile, "I got some information on the Wang house and the land it was built on."

The brothers turned to stare at their mom.

"You did?" said Joe.

"What was it, Mom?" Frank asked.

"I wrote it down somewhere," Mrs. Hardy replied. "The building that once stood on that spot did have something to do with pirates."

Pirates? Frank and Joe froze. Was it the Peg-Leg Inn?

# Chapter 8

# GOLLY ROGER

"Mom?" Joe asked slowly. "Was the building a place where pirates used to stay?"

"When they sailed into Bayport?" Frank added.

"I think I wrote it down here," Mrs. Hardy said. She reached into her jacket pocket, pulled out a note, and read it. "The place was called Pirate Pretzels. It was built in 1952 and torn down in 1978 to make room for more houses."

"Pretzels?" Frank said.

"1952?" Joe asked.

"Hey, I remember Pirate Pretzels!" Mr. Hardy said with a grin. "When I was a kid, I loved the chocolate-covered ones with nuts!"

"Unless that old pirate inn served pretzels, boys," Mrs. Hardy teased, "Jason has no ghosts in his house to worry about."

"Thanks, Mom, but how do we explain this?" Frank asked. He showed the pirate coin to his parents. "Jason found a bunch of these on his windowsill last night."

"May I see that?" Mr. Hardy asked. He took the coin from Frank and examined it.

"What do you think, Dad?" Joe asked.

"It looks like a pirate doubloon, but I'm not an expert," Mr. Hardy said. "Why don't you go to the Bayport Museum tomorrow? I'll bet the museum curators can tell you if the coin is authentic."

"And the museum is open on Sundays," Mrs. Hardy added.

"Great idea," Frank said.

"Yeah," Joe said. "But I hope it's not a real pirate coin."

"Why?" Mrs. Hardy asked.

"That would mean it was left by a real pirate ghost!" Joe replied with a gulp.

The next morning Frank and Joe rode their bikes to the Bayport Museum, which celebrated the town's seaport history.

"Wow, Frank," Joe said after walking through the door into the museum. "The last time I was here was on a class trip."

After getting their museum tickets, the brothers stopped to gaze at tall figureheads from ships, whale tusk carvings, a miniature model of Bayport from the 1700s, and a glass case filled with captains' logbooks.

"Look, Joe," Frank said, turning toward a large room filled with more glass cases. "That room has ancient coins inside. I saw it on my last class trip."

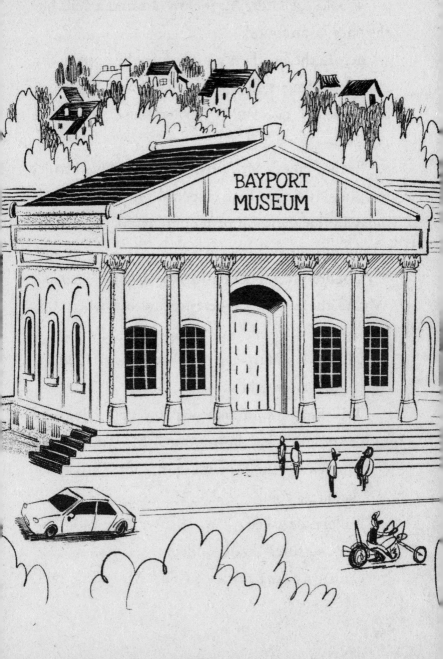

"Cool," Joe said. "Maybe we can find a coin like the ones Jason found."

Before the brothers could enter the coin room, a man wearing a dark suit walked over. His name badge read LEONARD TUTTLE, MUSEUM DIRECTOR.

"Hello, boys," Mr. Tuttle said. "I wanted to let you know that we have a special program for kids today in the auditorium. Would you like to attend? It's not too late!"

"Sounds great, but no, thank you," Frank replied. "My brother and I are here to find out where this came from."

Mr. Tuttle's mustache twitched as he studied the coin Frank showed him.

"We think it's an ancient pirate coin," Joe said with a smile. "What do you think, Mr. Tuttle?"

"Oh, it's a pirate coin, all right," Mr. Tuttle said. "A fake pirate coin."

"Fake?" Joe asked.

"Are you sure?" Frank added.

"This coin isn't made of gold," Mr. Tuttle said,

bending the coin just a bit. "It's made out of inexpensive metal."

The museum director smiled as he handed Frank the coin. "But it is an impressive replica," he said. "Bring it to school for show-and-tell."

"Show-and-tell?" Joe repeated as Mr. Tuttle walked away.

"He is the expert," Frank said. "And at least we know the coin didn't come from a pirate ghost."

"The coin may not be real," Joe explained, "but what about that creepy message in the blue bottle? And that pirate song someone taught Crackers—"

"Windy weather, boys, stormy weather, boys," a deep singing voice cut in. "When the wind blows, we're all together, boys!"

"You mean that song?" Frank asked slowly.

"That's the same song Crackers sang!" Joe said excitedly. He looked around. "But where's it coming from?"

Frank pointed down the hall. "It sounds like it's coming from down there!"

He and Joe followed the sound to a closed door marked AUDITORIUM. Joe opened the door a crack, and they peeked inside.

Sitting on the edge of the stage and singing to a bunch of kids was a man wearing a pirate hat and a black eye patch. An easel on the stage held a sign that read SALTY SEA SHANTIES BY PLUNDERIN' PETE!

"That pirate looks familiar!" Joe hissed to Frank. "It's Plunderin' Pete from the Pirate Palooza!"

"He's singing that song someone taught Crackers," Frank whispered.

"Maybe that someone," Joe whispered back, "was Plunderin' Pete!"

# Chapter 9

# ALL HANDS ON DECK!

Plunderin' Pete led the kids in a chorus of the song as Frank quietly shut the door.

"Do you think a singing pirate would scare Jason into believing in a ghost?" Frank asked.

"He did look disappointed after Jason told him he didn't believe in Captain Scurvydog's ghost," Joe said. "Maybe Plunderin' Pete wanted to make it look like his story was true."

All singing stopped. After a few seconds the

auditorium door swung open, backing the brothers against the wall. Peeking around the door, Frank and Joe saw kids filing out, each holding a bag. The bag was red with a Jolly Roger design on it.

"Jason got the same bag from Plunderin' Pete for winning the contest yesterday," Joe whispered.

"We never got to see what was inside," Frank pointed out.

Suddenly out walked Plunderin' Pete. He was soon greeted by Mr. Tuttle. Still behind the door, Frank and Joe listened in. . . .

"Thanks, Pete," Mr. Tuttle said. "The kids seemed to enjoy your show."

"The pleas-arrrgh was mine," Pete growled. "Now if you'll excuse me, Captain Scurvydog awaits."

"Frank!" Joe squeaked. "He said he's going to meet Captain Scurvydog. What do we do?"

"There's only one thing to do," Frank said as they watched Plunderin' Pete leave the museum. "Follow that pirate!"

By the time the brothers burst out of the museum, Plunderin' Pete's car was driving away.

"Are we sure it's Pete's car?" Frank asked.

"How many cars have Jolly Roger flags on them?" Joe said. "Let's go!"

Frank and Joe hopped onto their bikes. Keeping a safe distance, they trailed Plunderin' Pete's car to the Bayport Marina. From their bikes the boys watched Pete step out of the car to walk up the dock.

"He's heading toward one of the houseboats," Frank pointed out.

Pete stopped at one of the boats. Joe squinted to read the name painted on the hull. . . .

"It's called the *Captain Scurvydog*!" Joe exclaimed. "Plunderin' Pete named his houseboat after the pirate—or the pirate ghost."

The boys watched as Pete whipped off his pirate hat and cape. He tossed them onto the boat's deck, then walked up the dock back to his car.

"Are we lucky or what?" Joe said as the car zoomed off. "Now we can search the boat for coins and a blue bottle."

Frank shook his head and said, "I don't think so, Joe. If Plunderin' Pete lives on the boat, then—"

"Last one there is a rotten oyster!" Joe called back, charging up the dock.

Frank groaned as he followed Joe to the deck of the *Captain Scurvydog*.

"Let's go, Joe," he suggested as they looked around. "I don't want to walk the plank if Pete finds us snooping—"

"Wait!" Joe cut in. He pointed to a crate with the word TREASURE painted on the lid. "What could be in there?"

"Another treasure chest?" Frank said with a smirk. "Did Plunderin' Pete have a birthday party too?"

Joe was already lifting the lid to see what was inside. "More of Plunderin' Pete's red treasure bags," he reported. "A lot more."

"He must give away millions of those!" Frank said.

"Let's see what's inside once and for all," Joe suggested. He took out a bag and pulled out items one by one: a pirate eye patch, a plastic compass, a blue bottle—

"Blue bottle!" Frank exclaimed as he grabbed the awesome find.

"Yeah, but the bottle on Jason's doorstep didn't say *Pirate Pop*," Joe said, pointing out the label on the bottle.

"The label peels off," Frank said. "What else is in the bag?"

Joe flipped the bag upside down. Out onto the

deck dropped a music CD and a small pouch tied with a cord.

Frank picked up the pouch. He tugged the cord to open it and looked inside. That was when his jaw dropped.

"What? What's in it?" Joe asked.

"Coins," Frank answered excitedly as he spilled golden-colored coins from the pouch into his hand. "Check it out!"

Joe grabbed a coin. One side was stamped with a sailing ship. On the other side was a Jolly Roger flag— just like the coins Jason had found on his windowsill.

"It's a match!" Joe declared.

Frank's attention had turned to the CD. "Look at this," he told Joe. "It's called *Plunderin' Pete's Greatest Hits*."

"Pirate songs, coins, a blue bottle," Joe said, quickly writing the clues in their clue book. "Who else could have left those pirate things other than Plunderin' Pete?"

Frank narrowed his eyes thoughtfully. He looked up from the CD he was holding and said, "I think I know someone else who could have done all that."

Joe stared at his brother. If it wasn't Plunderin' Pete—who could it be?

# THE HARDY BOYS—and
# YOU!

## CAN YOU SOLVE THE MYSTERY OF THE PIRATE GHOST?

Grab a piece of paper and write your answers down. Or just turn the page to find out!

1. After looking inside the treasure bag, Frank thought of a new suspect. Who could he or she be? Write some possible suspects on a piece of paper.

2. Frank and Joe searched Plunderin' Pete's boat for pirate coins and a blue bottle. What other clues would you look for on his boat? Use a sheet of paper to write some possible clues.

3. Why did Plunderin' Pete's treasure bag turn out to be such a great clue? Write some reasons on a sheet of paper.

4. Which clues helped you to solve this mystery? Write them down.

# Chapter 10

# PIRATES AHOY!

"But the pirate stuff came from Plunderin' Pete's treasure bag," Joe said.

"And Jason got one of Pete's bags on Friday for winning the contest," Frank stated.

"Frank!" Joe gasped. "Are you saying Jason planted those pirate clues himself?"

"Maybe." Frank thought about it. "Jason could have taught Crackers an old pirate song from Pete's

CD. He could have peeled the label off the Pirate Pop bottle and stuffed in a message he wrote himself."

"Jason had coins from Pete's treasure bag too," Joe said. "But why would he want us to think a pirate ghost left those things?"

"I'm not sure," Frank admitted as he slipped the CD back into the bag. "All I know is that we have to get off this boat before—"

"Arrrgh, loitering landlubbers!" a deep voice growled.

The brothers froze. They'd know that voice anywhere. It was Plunderin' Pete's!

"If yer wanted a treas-arrrgh bag," Pete said as the boys turned around, "why didn't you lads just ask for one?"

"Sorry, Plunderin' Pete," Joe said, holding up the clue book. "My brother, Frank, and I are detectives."

"So we were looking for answers," Frank added.

"Answers?" Pete raised a brow above his eye patch. "To what question, me hearties?"

"Here's one," Frank said, lifting the treasure bag he and Joe had examined. "Is this the same bag you gave Jason Wang on Friday after he won the Talk Like a Pirate Contest?"

Pete nodded. "All my bags have the same treasures," he said. "It's a great way to promote my new CD!"

"Does your CD have the song we heard you sing at the museum before?" Joe asked. "The one about the blowy wind?"

"Aye!" Plunderin' Pete exclaimed. "That's one of my greatest hits!"

"Bingo," Joe said under his breath. If the song was on the CD, Jason could have taught it to Crackers!

"Now, then," Pete said. "Do you lads want a treas-arrrrgh bag?"

"We'll take this one, thanks," Frank said. "Then Joe and I will go."

"But not before I ask one more question," Joe told Pete. "Was there or was there not a Captain Scurvydog?"

Pete looked Joe straight in the eye and growled, "Dead men tell no tales."

Joe gulped, until Pete smiled and said, "But this

pirate does tell tales, and Captain Scurvydog is my favorite!"

"So he's not for real?" Joe asked.

"Shiver me timbers, no," Plunderin' Pete said. "Why do you think I call them tall tales?"

The brothers thanked Pete for his help and the treasure bag. As they walked to their bikes, Joe said, "This bag is filled with the best treasures we could find."

"You mean the eye patch?" Frank asked. "The compass?"

"The clues!" Joe declared happily.

The brothers pedaled straight to the Wang house. Jason stepped out onto the porch. His eyes widened when he saw the treasure bag in Frank's hand.

"Look familiar?" Joe asked.

"It's got a blue bottle, pirate coins," Frank said, "and a CD of old pirate songs."

"One of Crackers's new favorite songs is on it," Joe said. "The one about the blowy wind."

"The ghost of Captain Scurvydog taught Crackers that song!" Jason blurted.

"I'm sorry, Jason, but there was no Captain Scurvydog," Frank said gently. "Or his ghost. We talked to Plunderin' Pete, and he told us that the legend of Captain Scurvydog was a tall tale."

Jason stared at Frank and Joe. "I'd better go back inside," he said suddenly. "I have to cram for a science test tomorrow."

"It's spring break, Jason," Joe said. "No school tomorrow."

"Rats," Jason mumbled.

"Come on, Jason," Joe sighed. "We just want to know if you left those pirate ghost clues around the house."

"You got the same treasure bag on Friday," Frank pointed out. "You also had time to teach Crackers a new pirate song."

"Yo-ho-ho!" Crackers sang from his cage. "Blow the man down!"

"Two new songs," Joe said.

Jason shuffled his feet. He then heaved a big sigh and said, "I did teach Crackers that pirate song. I also put the fake pirate doubloons on my windowsill and wrote the message, too."

"How come, Jason?" Frank asked.

"Why would you want to trick us like that?" added Joe.

"Because I didn't want to dig up the treasure chest and make Captain Scurvydog mad," Jason admitted. "So I used stuff from Pete's treasure bag and wrote my own warning message."

Jason then cracked a smile and said, "I should have known that Frank and Joe Hardy would find out the truth!"

"It's okay, Jason," Frank said, smiling too. "Solving mysteries is what we do."

"And this mystery is totally solved!" Joe said, and wrote *Case Closed* in the clue book.

"Awesome!" Jason exclaimed. "Now that I know there's no Captain Scurvydog, I want to use the map I won to find the buried treasure."

"Can we still help?" Frank asked.

"You bet," Jason replied.

"In that case," Joe said as he traded high fives all around, "pirates ahoy!"

"Are you sure this is the place?" Jason asked. "Under this rock?"

It was later that day, and Joe was studying the treasure map. It had led him, Frank, and Jason to a spot near the snack stand in Bayport Park.

"*X* marks the spot!" Joe declared.

"What are we waiting for, mateys?" Frank said as he picked up the rock. "Let's start digging!"

Using his mom's gardening shovel, Jason dug a hole in the ground. He kept digging until his shovel hit something with a *clunk*.

"I found it, you guys!" Jason declared. "I found the treasure!"

The boys pulled out what looked like a pirate's old treasure chest. Jason spit on both hands, then popped open the lid.

"Cool," Frank said as they peered inside. The chest was filled with all kinds of things to have fun with.

"Thanks for helping me dig it up, guys," Jason told Frank and Joe, "and for telling me the truth about Captain Scurvydog."

Frank smiled as he pulled a plastic telescope from the chest. "No problem, Jason," he said, peering through the telescope. "The ghost of Captain Scurvydog may be fake, but this buried treasure . . . is the real deal!"